# DISNEP
# PIRATES of the CARIBBEAN
# JACK SPARROW

## The Age of Bronze

by Rob Kidd
Illustrated by Jean-Paul Orpinas

Based on the earlier life of the character, Jack Sparrow,
created for the theatrical motion picture,
*Pirates of the Caribbean: The Curse of the Black Pearl*,
screen story by Ted Elliott and Terry Rossio and Stuart Beattie and Jay Wolpert,
screenplay by Ted Elliott and Terry Rossio,
and characters created for the theatrical motion pictures
*Pirates of the Caribbean: Dead Man's Chest* and *Pirates of the Caribbean 3*
written by Ted Elliott and Terry Rossio

D0281101

Mr Kidd would like to thank Geoffrey Braswell for sharing his expertise in all things Mayan; Aaron, Nathan and Jenn fer readin'; Liz Rudnick for the beautiful amulet . . .

. . . and, of course, Liz Braswell and Rich Thomas for all their help rigging the ship.

Special thanks to Ken Becker.

This is a Parragon book
First published in 2007

Parragon
Queen Street House
4 Queen Street
Bath, BA1 1HE, UK

ISBN 978-1-4054-9062-7
Printed in UK

# The Age of Bronze

# CHAPTER ONE

The azure sea twinkled below a perfect sun. Welcoming beaches of soft, white sand skirted the coastline. Above the shore rose tall grey cliffs, dotted with rows of palm trees that swayed in the breeze. Little silver schools of fish leaped out of the water. For once, life was calm and good.

"This is what it's all about, mates," Jack Sparrow said, sighing. He stood at the rail of his boat, the *Barnacle*, taking in a deep breath of the salty air.

"Can't say it's unpleasant not to be on the run for once," first mate Arabella said in agreement. She tossed her auburn hair back and toasted the ocean with a raised golden goblet. Rubies sparkled along its rim.

Fitzwilliam P. Dalton III, a nobleman's son, ogled the cup and gave her a look.

"What?" she asked defensively. "It's only drinking water. I think I *deserve* a little special something after all we've been through. . . ."

"True enough, *mon ami*," Jean, another sailor, said, his green eyes twinkling. He clapped Fitzwilliam on the shoulder. "Leave Arabella alone. We all deserve 'a little special something' after our recent adventures, *non*?"

Constance, Jean's sister-turned-cat, meowed once in agreement, daintily cleaning one of her enormous, evil-looking, yellow claws.

"Yinb'ey pa wachoch," the Mayan sailor Tumen said, staring at the beach. Then he turned to the rest of his companions. "I'm going home," he translated.

"I haven't seen my home in over two years," Tumen continued. "I was kidnapped from my family by pirates. They took me right off the beach near our village. I was forced to work for them. I was sold from one ship to the next, including some of your *honourable* English ships." He gave Fitzwilliam a look. "I am glad to finally be free, and I've had a lot of fun with you, but all I've ever wanted to do is go home."

His eyes were wide and bright and he bit his lip, determined. But he was a little afraid to see how his crewmates would react.

"Point us in the right direction," Jack said with a grin and a bow. "We'll be glad to take you home."

*J*ust a few hours of easy sailing later, the *Barnacle* came to a small, protected bay. Piled here and there on the sands were carved grey boulders, covered in weathered inscriptions and designs. Behind the shore was a line of jagged hills. Perched along them was a cluster of huts, all facing the ocean. Columns of sweet-smelling smoke rose up from the village, but otherwise it was empty.

"No one's here!" Arabella said, surprised.

"Not very friendly relatives, eh?" Jack said, securing the anchor. "What'd you do to make them hide from you, mate?" Jack leaned in toward Arabella. "It's always the quiet ones you have to watch out for," he whispered.

"This is a European-style boat," Tumen pointed out. "The last time one came here, they kidnapped me and my cousins."

"Fascinating!" Fitzwilliam said, looking

through his spyglass. "I have always wanted to see a native village! Look at their primitive cooking fires!"

"Ahem." Arabella pushed the spyglass down, clearing her throat. "Ye might want to save yer anthropological observations for later, Master Dalton. This is Tumen's *family*. Can't ye show a little respect?"

Tumen hoisted himself over the side of the *Barnacle*, landing with a faint splash in the shallow water. "Heya!" he called.

Two heads peered out from behind the trunk of a palm tree. Cautiously, a little boy and girl eased themselves into the open, staring at the ship with untrusting eyes. Then the girl's face lit up. "Tumen!" she cried, running forward.

Tumen grinned and grabbed her, throwing her into the air and laughing. The little boy hugged Tumen's leg.

"Meet my brother and sister, Kan and K'ay," he said proudly.

More villagers began slowly emerging from the bushes and houses. They wore bright red-and-white clothes with colourful stripes woven into them. The women wore their hair up in thick black ropes braided with red-and-purple cords. Everyone grinned when they saw Tumen.

An old man stepped forward. He was almost completely bald and bent over, but carried himself with the dignity and strength of a leader. His robe was red and white like the rest of the villagers, but had a series of purple crosses down the middle. He wore a necklace of jade and gold that glittered in the sun.

"Mam!" Tumen cried. The old man held up his hand and said something back, smiling through crooked teeth. Tumen ran up the beach, grabbing the old man and hugging him.

"Who is this?" Fitzwilliam asked interestedly. "The witch doctor of your village?"

Tumen shook his head, still too happy to be annoyed at the very *wrong* term 'witch doctor'. "This is my great-grandfather, Mam."

"Oh, I just love family reunions," Jack said, clapping his hands together. "Now, where's the food?"

Arabella whacked him in the ribs.

"Mam, these are my friends," Tumen introduced, first in Mayan, then in English. "They are the only reason I ever made it back home."

The old man spoke, and his great-grandson translated. "He says this is an occasion for great celebration. The village will hold a ceremony tonight in my honour, and you are all invited to come. There will be dancing and feasting and storytelling."

"Dancing?" Fitzwilliam said, with a sidelong glance at Arabella. "I would be most pleased if I could escort you tonight, my lady." He made a little bow and held out his hand. Despite herself, Arabella fairly glowed.

"Absolutely not," Jack snapped. "As captain of this ship, *I* should be the one to take her. To protect her from you and the rest of these . . ." He waved his hand searching for the word. ". . . *scallywags* what sail aboard the *Barnacle*. I do have rank to pull, you know."

"Come now, Jack," the future Earl of Dalton said. "You would not know how to dance the waltz. Surely."

"And of course we can all just see *you* getting down with the natives like their best mate," Jack shot back. "You *might* get your beloved boots and trousers dirty."

Arabella cleared her throat. The two boys

8

stopped their arguing and turned. She had her hand on Jean's arm. The Creole boy was smiling wickedly.

"Mind ye two, I have already decided to go with Jean," she announced. "He's the one not acting like a total dolt, if ye hadn't noticed."

Jean gave a little mock bow to Jack and Fitzwilliam. "I give you permission to take my sister, *mon capitan*. You can protect *her*."

Jack glared at Constance.

Tumen just rolled his eyes.

# CHAPTER TWO

That night, the villagers built a huge bonfire on the beach. Giant logs were rolled up to sit on. The five crewmates of the *Barnacle* watched as dancers performed a rite of thankfulness. Jade and shell bracelets clacked in time to the music as the dancers stomped their feet. The lead wore a colourful headdress covered in feathers. Torches planted in the sand cast eerie shadows around his face. Men and women in the audience chanted along.

"You must admit, this *is* fascinating," Fitzwilliam whispered to Arabella.

"It's a lot of fun, I'll grant ye that," Arabella conceded.

Bowls of corn soup were passed around, as were tortillas stuffed with boiled eggs. Cooked manioc was served on leaves. Platters of fish garnished with oysters were set before them. Seabirds were roasted whole and served with avocado.

"This here meal is mighty tasty, mate," Jack said, chewing happily. "What do you call this, then?"

"Xoloitzcuintli," Tumen said with a faint smile.

"That some kind of rabbit or bird or something?"

"It is a small, hairless dog."

Jack choked, spitting out what was in his mouth.

Tumen and Jean laughed.

"I'm going to miss you, *mon frere*," Jean said with a brave smile, putting his arm around Tumen. "We've been through a lot together."

"I could not have survived it without you," Tumen admitted.

Constance rubbed up against Tumen's leg, purring loudly. "I'm going to miss you, too," he said, scratching her under the chin.

Giant stone mugs of chocolate were passed around. Arabella was delighted with the dessert and wound up drinking hers *and* Jean's. And part of Jack's. Then the villagers and the crew gathered around the fire. Tumen told the story of his adventures aboard the *Barnacle*. After that, he translated while his older brother, Chila, told the story of Tumen's kidnapping. Other people told tales about their heroes' gods. When Mam cleared his voice and tapped his cane on the ground, everyone was silent for his turn.

"He is telling a story about the greatest treasure mankind has ever known," Tumen explained in a whisper.

"Is it cursed?" Jack asked drily. "Any cursed *people* guarding it? Cursed *ingots* that minted it, cursed *cats* that claim to be its sister? Because as you know, I've sworn off anything involving magic and curses. Give me a nice buried treasure chest. Pirate's loot. An unlocked bank. Something *simple*."

Mam shook his head at Jack. "This is a treasure not to be sought out," Tumen translated. "It is a City of Gold."

"El Dorado!" Fitzwilliam said, perking up. "I have heard of the place. The Spanish lost many men in expeditions sent looking for it. An utter waste of resources," he said dismissively.

13

Tumen translated Mam's response: "Not El Dorado. This is something far greater. This is another city."

"Well, where is it, man, I mean, *Mam*?" Jack said, frustrated. "It sounds like a right fine place to visit."

Mam's black eyes grew unreadable as he looked at Jack. He spoke quietly. Tumen looked at him questioningly, then said it in English. "'Wherever the silver lives, the city is.'"

A hush fell over the crowd; even the insects in the brush seemed to fall silent. The crew of the *Barnacle* shivered.

The evening was soon over. Villagers began to get up and go inside, retreating from the cold of the night. The bonfire died down to red and orange embers that glowed feebly against the blackness of the sea and the sky. Fitzwilliam gave Arabella his jacket, and she pulled it tightly around her shoulders.

"'Wherever the silver lives, the city is,'" she murmured softly. "What do you think that means?"

"Perhaps it is a town near a silver mine," Fitzwilliam suggested. "Maybe 'living' is just another way of saying 'being mined'."

"That is so . . . unpoetic," Jean objected. "Maybe it means that everyone who seeks it out has precious metal on the brain, like it's all they think about. So they all disappear, and wind up together in this lost City of Gold."

"And maybe," Jack interrupted, "it's just – oh, and this one will be hard to believe, mates, I'm sure – far, far too complicated . . . Maybe it's a city. Made. Of. Gold." His eyes grew wide and distant, imagining not just roads paved with gold, but buildings built of it, and statues. Even things like chairs and tables.

"Remember what Mam said," Tumen

reminded them, noticing the glow in their eyes. "It is not to be sought out."

But despite this warning, all of them – even Tumen – grew drowsy and fell asleep on the white sands of the Yucatán, dreaming of a golden town.

# CHAPTER THREE

The sun had just begun to warm its way through the night's chill when the crew of the *Barnacle* was woken by a commotion.

They opened their eyes to see the people of Tumen's village shouting and running – mainly in their direction. One young man took the lead. He had a sharp nose and fierce black eyes, and something that looked suspiciously like a short spear in his hand. Jack's eyes popped open.

"Oh, what now? Can I not have a moment's rest?" Jack said.

The boy with the spear was called Yaxun. Tumen frowned. The two boys had never got on, even in the best times.

"What has happened?" Tumen asked.

"You – you lead this filthy crew here – especially that particularly filthy one with the rag on his head – and look what happened!" Yaxun shouted. "Or maybe it was *you* who stole the amulet. You dress like them now. You might as well be one of them!"

"*Amulet*? Not the Sun-and-Stars?" Tumen asked, hoping it wasn't true.

"Yes, the Sun-and-Stars amulet," an old woman said sorrowfully. "The same one the last of the Xitami entrusted to us before Cortés and his men wiped them out. We kept it safe for many years – since before my great-grandmother's mother. And now it is gone."

"And it disappears the same night you bring your friends here!" Yaxun said accusingly, pointing at the crew with his spear.

"There has been some mistake," Tumen protested. "Let me speak with Mam."

Yaxun sneered. "Oh, yes, go and speak to him. You will not be happy with what you find. Or perhaps you will. Who can say?"

"Wait here. Do not move," Tumen told the crew.

"Wouldn't think of it, mate," Jack said, getting ready to take a step to run for the *Barnacle*. But he quickly checked himself, noticing that many of the men had begun to pull out their spears.

Tumen raced over the sands to Mam's house. He was sure it was a mistake; Mam would help clear it up. But when he got to his great-grandfather's hut, he could already tell something was wrong. Incense poured

19

out of the windows in clouds, and Chila squatted outside, shaking his head and scattering flower petals. When he looked up and saw Tumen, he just shook his head sadly.

"Mam is very sick. . . I believe it is something to do with the men you brought here."

"No! It can't be!" Tumen forced his way in. There, in the dark, curled up on a mat, was his great-grandfather. Several villagers tended to him, with bowls of broth. They laid cool, wet cloths on his brow.

"He has a fever," Tumen's grandmother said. She narrowed her eyes at him and almost spat. "I think you should go."

Tumen staggered back, stunned at the force of her anger. All of them – all his family, who he had missed for so long and whom he was so overjoyed to finally see – all of them looked at him with *hate* in their eyes.

Yaxun was waiting for him outside, the crowd of armed men behind him.

"The council of elders has agreed," he said, sneering. "You are to be expelled from the village, never to return."

"No – it's a mistake–" Tumen began. He looked at each of his old friends, the people he had grown up with. Every one of them either looked away or met his eye with disgust.

With his head hung low, Tumen headed back to the beach. He turned back once to see his little brother and sister in tears.

What possibly could have happened? Maybe someone had misplaced the amulet? Unlikely, after keeping it safe for so long. It was more than a little strange that it disappeared the same night that he returned, but it couldn't have had anything to do with him or his friends.

Could it?

After all, how well did he really know any of them, anyway?

They all *seemed* nice enough, and he had been on some great adventures with them . . . but except for Jean, he wasn't really that close to any of them. Fitzwilliam was just an uptight rich guy, as far as he could tell. And crazy, too. Who leaves a comfy noble life to become a wandering adventurer? Arabella was friendly, if a bit quick-tempered and hot-headed. But she used to work at a tavern filled with pirates and cut-throats. Could she be one, too? And then there was Jack . . . Jack was just plain odd.

By the time he reached the dying bonfire, Tumen was furious.

"Give it back!" he demanded, planting himself inches from Jack's face.

"Um, give *what* back, mate?" Jack asked,

cautiously glancing quickly to his left and right.

"The amulet! I know you took it! Give it back!" Tumen tightened his hands into fists.

"What are ye talking about?" Arabella asked. "What is Jack supposed to have taken?"

"One of you took it!" Tumen whirled around, glaring at her and Fitzwilliam. "One of you took the Sun-and-Stars amulet. My people have protected it for hundreds of years and it just *happens* to have disappeared last night! *NOW, WHERE IS IT?*"

# CHAPTER FOUR

"*H*ere now! I rather resent your implications, implying that I was implicit and whatnot," Jack said, waving his hands frantically. "I don't know anything about an amulet, much less *had* anything to do with taking one. Besides, had there been an amulet, I would have had to have known there had been an amulet in order to have taken an amulet what was there to be taken. Savvy?"

"I am forced to agree with Jack this one time," Fitzwilliam said frostily, bracing his legs in the white sand. "How could you mistrust your own crew, your own friends, after all we have been through together?"

"Besides, Jack *couldn't* have taken it," Arabella said, shooting a sneer at Jack. "He was right here all night. He snores like a pig. I barely slept at all."

Jean put his arm around Tumen's shoulders. "Come now, *mon ami*. Tell us what has made you so upset."

Tumen sank to the ground, burying his face in his hands. He felt like crying. "They have expelled me forever. From my own home. They think I led you here to steal it. And – Mam is sick, and they blame me for that, too."

"Expelled you? Forever?" Jean said with horror. Constance hissed angrily.

"Tell us about this amulet," Arabella suggested soothingly.

"And why it's so great that I would have stolen it," Jack added.

Tumen sighed. "No one knows exactly what it is. . . it is supposed to be very powerful. We think the Xitami people acquired it from the Spanish. The Xitami wanted to make certain it never landed in their hands again. They did not tell our ancestors what it did, only to keep it safe." He started to draw in the sand as he spoke. "The amulet is made of a white metal that is not silver. It has three hollow settings. The three missing gems were said to be lost long ago, before my people came into possession of it."

The five crewmates looked at the drawing morosely.

"Well, of course we've got to go and find it," Jack decided. "We'll get it back, return it to the village and clear your good name. You can go home again, and we can be on our way."

It wasn't just a good deed he would be doing . . . there was something in it for Jack, too. Returning the amulet was also a way to form some very powerful allies in the Yucatán. A useful thing for a sailing adventurer in search of treasure and safe harbours. On the other hand, right now with this amulet missing, he had some pretty powerful enemies.

"Well, what are you waiting for?" Jack shouted, sweeping his hands forward. "Go look around! See if we can find this thing, or at least some clues."

The crew split up and took different sections of the area around the bay, being careful not to come too close to the village. What seemed like an impossible task ended sooner than anyone thought it might. A bright piece of cloth among the green leaves of the jungle caught Jack's attention. His eyes grew wide and he brought everyone to the small clearing where he stood.

"Feast your eyes on this, lads and lassie and lassie-cat-thing," he said, a little smugly.

There, sitting at the base of a tree between two roots as if it had been placed carefully, was their clue.

"It's a little doll," Arabella said with wonder, reaching for it.

It was little more than two sticks crossed and wrapped in cloth, built up to make a body and head. The head had no hair, but the face had a stitched mouth and eyes. It was dressed in a strangely familiar red-and-white cloth with purple crosses down the middle . . . and had a miniature jade necklace around its neck.

"Look at the clothes it wears!" Tumen exclaimed, picking it up. "Those are Mam's robes!"

Jean took the creepy little figure and looked at it grimly. "It is a doll made by someone who practises *magicks*." He pulled the doll's clothes apart at the chest. Over where the heart would have been was a drawing in blood-red ink: a crescent dagger with a serpent wrapped around it. Jean let out a low whistle. "Ooh. We're in for it, now. This is the sign of Madame Minuit – Madam Midnight – of New Orleans. This is her doing."

"Like Tia Dalma?" Jack asked. "A practitioner of the mystical arts, as they say?"

Jean nodded. "She is a very, very powerful woman. But she only uses her powers for her own profit. This could be why your great-grandfather is sick, Tumen. She is using this doll to *make* him sick."

"Why would anyone do that?" Tumen asked, exasperated. "Mam has never done anything bad to anyone. He has never been to New Orleans. He has never been out of the *Yucatán*!"

"I don't know, but I'll bet that maybe, just *maybe*, this precious amulet you keep going on and on about has something to do with it," Jack pointed out sarcastically. "Why must I always need to state the obvious to you people?"

Tumen blinked. The connection *was* obvious. The disappearance of the amulet, Mam suddenly becoming sick . . . the doll couldn't have been a coincidence. He turned and went back to the village. The others followed.

"I've got to see Mam," Tumen protested when Yaxun tried to stop him.

"I am sorry," Tumen's older brother, Chila, said sadly, also blocking his way. "But if you try to come back again we will need to turn you and your friends away – forcefully. Please go – and take with you the evil that has invaded our village. You are not my brother any longer. They have changed you."

# CHAPTER FIVE

A pale half-moon rose over the midnight sea as the *Barnacle* made its way through the Gulf of Mexico towards New Orleans. Thousands of stars added to its ghostly light, causing the tips of waves to glow an eerie white. The dark water blended into the night sky. A lone, lost gull cried once overhead.

"I'm so worried about Mam," Tumen said. "He was so sick. At his age, the fever is deadly. . ."

"Ah, do not worry, Tumen!" Jean assured

his friend, clapping a hand on his shoulder. "The doll will only work while in the hands of whoever made it. This little doll was dropped in the sands, lost. Its power has been severed. Your great-grandfather is feeling better already."

Arabella raised an eyebrow at Jean over Tumen's head. Was the Creole boy telling the truth or just saying something to make Tumen feel better?

Jean nodded vigorously, fingers over his heart.

"A fine night for sailing," Fitzwilliam said, changing the subject.

"I don't agree," Arabella said, shaking her head. "It feels . . . cursed, somehow."

"Bup-bup-bup-bup!" Jack ordered, taking a hand off the wheel to wave a finger at his two mates. "No curses, no magic, no more!"

"No *curses*, Jack? Well, what do you call this, then?" Jean asked sarcastically, holding up the doll.

"A terribly unfortunate set of coincidental hardships," Jack suggested, but warily kept one eye on the doll. Jean wiggled it at him, then tossed it at the captain of the *Barnacle*. Jack jumped out of the way and let out a high-pitched yelp, still keeping hold of the wheel. He shot Jean a dirty look.

"What is *that*?" Tumen asked, pointing out over the sea.

It was hard to make out at first. Just a random darkness blocking out some stars on the horizon. It could have been a trick of the light or a passing cloud. But as the *Barnacle* sailed silently toward it, the blackness in the sky grew bigger and bigger.

"It's a ship," Jack realized first. But there was something terribly wrong with it. For one thing, it was dead in the water. *Dead.* Barely moving with the swells and waves. It was hardly rocking. Not like a ship at all. There were no sounds coming from it, not even the cracking of sails in the wind. And not a single light shone from its deck or its cabins. Even the water around it was unnaturally still.

Constance leaped onto the railing and sniffed curiously in the ship's direction.

"Some ship," Arabella whispered.

"I'll just tack us to port, get a better look," Jack decided, spinning the wheel. No one objected, but then again, no one sounded very enthusiastic, either. "Oh, don't all cheer at once for your heroic captain," Jack said sarcastically.

As they came around the side of the ghostly ship, the bowsprit gleamed in a way that wood – even freshly painted wood –

usually doesn't. But it wasn't until they saw moonlight hit the hull full on that the crew of the *Barnacle* realized what was wrong.

"It's made of *metal*," Arabella whispered.

From bow to stern, from poop deck to top-sail, everything glowed dully under the moon.

"Impossible," Fitzwilliam said slowly. "An entire metal ship? It would never be able to float!"

"And yet, there it is, mate," Jack said, squinting. "Bronze, it looks like."

"Look – the water," Jean pointed. The waves around the base of the ship weren't just unnaturally still. They were solid metal, too. A whole skirt of metal water surrounded the ship.

"Maybe it's some kind of sculpture," Arabella suggested tentatively, knowing it was stupid even as she said it. But she could think of no other rational explanation. "Maybe to commemorate a battle at sea?"

Jean and Tumen shook their heads. "No, we have been in and out of the port at New Orleans many, many times," the Creole boy said. "Even if the British or Spanish or French made something like this, we would have seen it or heard about it."

Jack made a decision. "Take the wheel, Fitzy."

Jack put an extra knife in his belt and wrapped a length of rope around his waist. He was going over to the ship. And as he stared at his crew, it was clear none of them would be helping him.

He snarled at the crew and, grabbing another rope, leaped over the side of the *Barnacle* onto the metal water below . . . which cracked beneath him!

Like ice, the metal plates snapped under

Jack's weight. Unlike ice, the moment a piece broke off it sank quickly and heavily into the water.

With a scream Jack leaped again, flipping himself into the air and closer to the bronze ship. The metal water was thicker there and supported his weight. But the metal that touched the real water was blue and scaly. He reached down and easily broke off a piece.

He looked at it curiously, then tossed it aside. He had to be more careful. Then he undid the rope at his waist and threw it up and up until a loop at the end hooked around the lowest spar on the mizzenmast. He pulled it a few times, making sure it was firmly caught, then scurried up it. He didn't look down; falling and landing on metal 'water' would surely kill him.

At the top, Jack grabbed the rail and hoisted

himself over. His boots hit the deck with a dull *clang*, not the *clunk* wooden boards would have made. He knocked on the rail – it made the same noise. So did a barrel sitting to the side. So did the ropes. He peered at them closely. Every fibre, every kink and knot and hair was made of solid metal.

"If Bell is right, whoever did this was a brilliant sculptor," Jack said. "I'll need to find him, as I'd love him to decorate the estate I will one day inherit from whatever rich old widow decides to bestow her property to this charming, good-looking captain."

A looming shape near the wheel of the ship cast a long, ominous shadow on the deck. Jack swallowed hard, then sneaked over to the wheel.

Jack's eyes grew wide.

"Oh, this is not normal at all," he said.

A bronze man was standing at the wheel.

Every detail was perfect, from the hair on his head to the fingernails on his hands. He was staring at something beyond Jack, on the other side of the ship. His face was frozen in horror, as if he had been screaming.

Jack shivered. Then he made a fist and rapped on the fellow's head. "Anybody home?"

Searching the ship turned up the rest of the crew, also metal.

"Cheery lot," Jack said. Except for the man at the wheel, everything seemed completely normal. But metal. It didn't look like anything traumatic had happened. No fights had broken out. Nothing on board the ship was unusual in the slightest – except for the ship and the crew themselves.

It was in the captain's cabin that things began to hint of what went wrong. On the floor, the captain himself was frozen on his hands and knees, hand to his throat. His eyes popped out of their sockets. He looked ill, or as if he was being tortured. But there wasn't anything around his neck, nor were there visible wounds on him. Not a drop of blood – bronze or otherwise.

And then Jack found the doll.

Even though it was just sticks and rags and bits of things – all bronze – it sat on the bunk, placed on the pillow.

"Either the captain has one very creepy little girl running around on board his ship, or this is another one of those odd little doll things," Jack said, picking it up. Closer inspection revealed that it was dressed just like the metal captain – down to a scrawny feather in its cap. Jack stuffed it into his belt.

"Why?" he muttered to himself, going

back to the deck and swinging down the rope. "Why is it *always* magic and curses and metal ships and weird little dolls?"

He leaped over the side of the *Barnacle* with a typical Jack flourish.

"Did you find anything?" Arabella asked anxiously.

"Just a bunch of metal lads and metal sails. Nothing worth taking. And *this*," he tossed the doll at Jean. The other boy almost dropped it, unprepared for its weight. "It seems the poor things were *turned* into metal. This was a *real* ship, and something terrible happened to it."

"Look." Jean turned the doll over. On its foot was the now-familiar dagger and snakes. "Again, the mark of Madame Minuit."

"What could she possibly have wanted with this ship?" Fitzwilliam said. "It does not even appear to be carrying much cargo."

The crew was getting closer to New Orleans and the clues just kept building up. But they had a feeling that answers would await them in the Crescent City.

# CHAPTER SIX

As dawn broke, the city of New Orleans appeared on the horizon. It was as though it had risen up out of the water – appeared out of nowhere. There was a certain magic to the town, even from afar.

No one had slept well since coming across the big metal ship and the tiny bronze doll. But now the crew, especially Jean, was in high spirits.

"Ah! *Nouvelle-Orleans!* How I have missed you!" he cried. Constance mewed in agreement.

"Just so ye know, Jack," Arabella said, sliding up to him, "I'm pleased we've been takin' Tumen and Jean to their homes – but don't feel a need to return me to Tortuga anytime soon."

"Likewise," Fitzwilliam said with feeling.

Jack just rolled his eyes. "Yes, yes, very well," he said dismissively. He needed most of his concentration to steer them into the harbour: it was a much busier one than he was used to. All sorts of ships, from sloops to frigates, from fishing boats to man-o'-wars, crowded the waters. It took some doing to find a convenient slip close to the city's centre, up the river a little way.

"All ashore that's going ashore . . . and remember where we parked," Jack said with a grin, straightening his bandana. According to Jean, it was a short walk from the dock to the back alleys of the French

Quarter. All they had to do was start asking around, show the doll and get some questions answered. Easy stuff.

So, of course, the trouble began immediately.

"*Halte!*"

A man in a smart uniform marched up the dock to the *Barnacle*. He was flanked by two muscled men in slightly less smart uniforms.

"The *gendarme* – the police," Jean said. "With a port official."

"What is all this, then?" the first man asked in French, then repeated in heavily accented English. He had a sharp little nose and squinty little eyes. Just the sort of man who enjoyed bureaucracy and making trouble for perfectly honest adventurers.

"Excuse me, good sir," Jack said, sweeping his cap off as he bowed. "We're just here for a bit of pleasure . . . seeing your fine city, its lovely restaurants . . . we're just tourists, really. No trouble for you at all."

"Where are your papers?" the official demanded, shaking his hand at them. "This is a commercial port – you have to have your papers to dock."

"Well, we *would* have papers, kind sir, except we're not – as you can see – a commercial vessel," Jack pointed out, raising an eyebrow in the direction of the *Barnacle*. He had to think fast. Getting into a row with the local police as soon as they came ashore was *not* a good way to *quietly* look for the powerful Madame Minuit. He leaned over and spoke confidentially to the official. "I didn't want to have to *tell* you this, 'cause I'm not *supposed* to, but we're *actually* on a *secret* mission transporting a *powerful member* of the French aristocracy."

The official gave him a sceptical look.

"Oh, yes, I am *sure* a French nobleman would travel aboard such a . . . a . . . *fishing* boat with such a crew," he said, waving his hand dismissively.

Unfortunately, Jack had to admit that the *Barnacle* didn't really look like an aristocrat's ship. The beams were all warped, where it *had* paint it was peeling, and the whole thing reeked of ancient fish.

None of them looked like French aristocracy, either. Tumen definitely didn't. Arabella was pretty enough to pass for a duchess, but her dress was worn, and she stood and glared like, well, a tavern girl. Jean spoke fluent French, but he looked about as aristocratic as Bell. And Fitzwilliam . . .

Well, actually, in his somehow-still-pristine blue jacket, gleaming sword at his side, Fitz really did look the part. Jack nodded desperately at him.

Fitzwilliam understood immediately. He stepped forward, shoulders back, head high, classic disdain on his face.

"*Bonjour*, Monsieur," he began in flawless French.

Jean whispered, translating for Jack, Tumen and Arabella. Jack shooed him away, as if to say he didn't *need* a translator.

"What is the holdup? I *demand* to be let ashore at once!" Fitzwilliam continued.

"Excuse me, Monsieur 'Nobleman'," the official said, no more polite than before. "Please enlighten me as to why you are travelling in such . . . conditions. And without papers."

"I am a cartographer in the employ of the King himself," Fitzwilliam said smoothly. "I was sent here to complete the survey of the territory in Louisiana we have rightfully taken back from the Spanish. My ship here was set upon by pirates – I believe I am the sole survivor. These lowly, er . . ." he looked at his friends, ". . . fisherpersons saved my life and are escorting me upriver until a replacement crew and ship are sent."

The official sniffed and shook his head.

"I have had no word of any royal ship that was commandeered by pirates, or any such map-making expedition!"

"Have you heard any news from court at all, then?" Fitzwilliam shot back. "Please do not tell me that His Majesty's messenger ship was lost as well!"

"A likely story – first your ship is lost, then the mail boat," the agent sneered. But his men were beginning to look unsure.

"Do you want to bring down the anger of the throne upon you?" Fitzwilliam demanded frostily.

The port agent considered it. On the *very* remote possibility the young man before him wasn't lying, he and his men might face the guillotine if they didn't let him through. Or at least receive a reprimand and a demotion. And besides, look at the rest of them – at worst, they were a bunch of young sailors come to New Orleans for some fun. What harm could they do?

"All right," the port agent said, "you are free to go. But move your mighty *Barnacle* to the far end of the port – I cannot have a vile old fishing boat here."

He even saluted Fitzwilliam – just in case.

"*Merci*," Jack said, saluting him back.

"That was fantastic, Fitz," Arabella said, hugging him. The noble boy kept his stoic expression, but blushed.

"I had no idea you spoke French so well," Jean laughed, slapping him on the back.

"You didn't make too bad a hash of it," Jack conceded. "Now, let's go and bring the mighty *Barnacle* to the other side of the port and finally disembark!"

$\mathcal{T}$he harbourmaster turned out to be just the beginning of their problems. The sun that had risen so pleasantly on their destination that morning now beat down on them unmercifully, despite the soft sky. The air itself was hot and wet, and walking through it was like taking a steam shower. With a fur coat on. Next to a hot furnace. In August.

"I'm used to the heat of the islands," Arabella said, pushing the hair back from her face. "But it's nothing like *this*. Ow!" She slapped her elbow. The mosquitoes were buzzing around them in full force.

Jack already had several nasty bites on his neck. "I'll take honest old Caribbean

bed lice over these winged beasties any day,"
he growled, waving his hands in the air, trying to shoo them away.

"I only hope we do not get malaria,"
Fitzwilliam muttered.

Jean was still in high spirits. He pointed
out familiar sights, nostalgic places, interest-
ing features. Cobbled streets and wrought-
iron balconies. Brightly painted houses and
shuttered windows. And people . . . people
from all over the world, in all different kinds
of dress. From mourning widows to real
French noble ladies in bright silks. And
the men here weren't *all* pirates, as they
were in Tortuga. There seemed to be a pretty good mix of merchants, tradesmen,
sailors, businessmen, dockworkers, pesky
French officials . . .

. . . and more priests, street-corner magicians, mystics and tea-leaf readers than

seemed possible for one city. Some wore colourful, flowing garb and carried crystal balls. Some had the tattered, muddy dress of mystics who lived in the swamps and sported chains of skulls around their necks like the famous soothsayer Tia Dalma. Some were covered in beads and jewellery, clacking as they walked. Their cries were deafening.

"Potions, potions for sale! Help you find love!"

"Spells and curses for the needy . . ."

"Protection charms! Sailors' knots! Will keep you safe at sea!"

An ancient woman, dark-eyed and bent, ran up to Arabella and made a croaking, cackling noise. Without warning, the crone threw a handful of something at her and screamed.

Arabella's hands flew to her face. When

the *things* clattered to the street like tiny bones she realized what they were.

"Chicken feet!" she cried disgustedly. She jumped back from the pile of shrivelled and curled-up claws.

But Constance happily began to nose through the pile, chewing on them.

A pockmarked man with a low-brimmed hat drawn down to hide his face grabbed Fitzwilliam by the arm and fanned cards in his face.

"Read the pretty boy his fortune?" he suggested nastily. His breath stank of rot and decay, his eyes were dark.

"Ah – no, thank you," Fitzwilliam said, pulling his eyes away from the hypnotic designs on the cards.

A young girl in a simple blue dress tugged on Jack's trousers. But when he bent down to listen, her voice was cracked and ancient, and her eyes were those of an old woman. One who had seen too much. Jack recoiled disgustedly.

"Monsieur? I can help you," she hissed. She leaned forward and whispered into his ear, motioning toward Constance. "*I can turn you into a cat, so you can become a little more friendly with your mate over here.*"

"No, thank you," Jack said, sneering, straightening his back and walking on.

"Jean, my friend," Jack said, leaning in closely. "Are *any* of these fascinating characters the lovely Madame Minuit for whom we are so desperately searching?"

Jean shuddered. "No, *mon ami*. As . . . disturbing as they are, *Madame* is far worse."

Jack sighed and looked around. Fitzwilliam was fending off a girl who was trying to sell him love charms. Arabella was trying to convince an albino Cajun that she was *not* interested in purchasing the eye of a dead voodoo priest. Constance was hissing, in a stand-off with an all-white cat with white eyes.

"I think the best place to look for her is – " Jean stopped in the middle of what he was saying. There was a strange look on his face. His eyes went blank, as if he were in a trance. He took a deep breath and didn't blink but stared straight ahead.

"That's done it, then," Jack said, shaking his head. "Our only native guide has fallen under a spell."

# CHAPTER SEVEN

Arabella and Fitzwilliam finally managed to shake off the vendors hounding them. When they made their way back to Jack, they found him glaring at a motionless Jean, whose eyes were glazed.

"Oh, my stars," Arabella said, alarmed. "What happened to *him*?"

"*Who* happened to him?" Fitzwilliam demanded, indicating the strange people all around them.

"I haven't the foggiest," Jack said dismissively, waving his hands and snapping his fingers in Jean's face.

Jean took several deep breaths and blinked slowly. It was as if he were coming out of a deep sleep, or surfacing after too much time underwater.

"Andouille . . ." he said softly.

"What? Who might that be?" Jack asked, looking around. "Is she responsible for this?"

"Filé . . . étouffée . . ." the boy continued, dazed.

"I think the poor lad is talking about food . . . again,"* Arabella realized with a smile. "Andouille is a kind of sausage."

The wind had shifted, and the smells of spicy noontime meals wafted over the square. Restaurants and taverns were cooking oysters, crayfish and jambalaya for hungry crowds.

* The crew first discovered Jean's love for epicurean delights in Vol. 3: *The Pirate Chase*.

"Jean!" Jack said, exasperated. He whacked the boy around the head. "Get your head out of the gumbo pot. We're on a *mission* here."

"*Oui, oui, of course,*" Jean said, shaking his head to clear it. "But it has just been so long. . . ."

"We'll tend to your homesick stomach in just a moment," Jack promised, rolling his eyes. "Now, tell me, if none of *these* wretches and hooligans be your dreaded Madame Minuit, where else could we look? Has she set up shop on another street?"

Jean shook his head, still distracted. "Madame Minuit does not solicit on the street. She does not have to. No one knows precisely where her hideout is – they say it moves around. We will have to work hard to find her . . ."

Before Jack could get another question in,

Jean took another deep breath of the delicious air. He looked anxiously towards the stalls across the way, where plumes of brown smoke and the bubble and pop of simmering stews held his full attention.

Arabella put a hand to her stomach. "I'm a wee bit hungry, too, Jack," she admitted.

"All right," the captain of the *Barnacle* sighed, pushing his hat back. "We should ruminate and digest some victuals, then, before we begin this search for the elusive witch doctress."

Jean's eyes sparkled. "Come with me, my friends! I promise you will eat food like you have never tasted before!"

Fitzwilliam and Jack exchanged looks, shrugging, and they all followed Jean as he made a beeline for one stall in particular. It looked even tattier and more questionable than the others. A giant man with wild silver-and-white hair stirred a giant iron pot over a fire.

Jean held up a coin and tossed it into the air. Without taking his other hand off the giant wooden spoon, the big man caught it and stuffed it into his pocket. Then he pulled out a dirty-looking bowl and filled it, handing it to Jean without ever looking at him.

Jack waited politely for the boy to offer it around first, but instead Jean dived right in, slurping from the side of the bowl like a pig.

He didn't stop.

The rest of the crew watched him with widening eyes. He ate the whole thing – and licked the bottom – seemingly without taking a breath. When he finished, he had smears of food around his mouth and bits dripping from his cheeks. Fitzwilliam turned away in disgust. Constance licked at the drops on the ground.

"*Je regrette . . .*" Jean apologized, wiping his face. "But it is too good to share."

"It smells delicious," Arabella said tactfully, handing him her handkerchief. "What is it?"

"Alligator stew, the best in Creole country," he replied, grinning.

Arabella turned white. Fitzwilliam couldn't hide a look of horror on his face. Tumen looked faintly ill.

"Right! Alligator stew all around, then, *garçon*," Jack said, clapping his hands together quickly. "Four in your finest soiled little bowls."

Constance growled threateningly.

"All right, *five*," Jack conceded. "But I'm not paying the tip."

The crew of the *Barnacle* took their lunch over to a low stone wall where they could perch and eat in relative comfort.

Other people were eating lunch as well. Most were sailors, locals, and dockworkers, talking politics or about the ships that had come in. The hum of French, Cajun, English and Spanish buzzed around them. The scent of Creole spices hung thick in the air.

And then something piqued Jack's attention. He was especially attuned to anything that sounded scheming, plotting or potentially illegal.

"*Do you have it? Did you get it from the ship?*"

"*Yes. And it is in place now.*"

This sounded good.

Jack not-so-casually turned himself so he could get a look at the conspirators. He pretended to concentrate on his stew and watched them over the rim of his bowl.

The first one who spoke was an old man dressed in long, tattered robes. And snakes.

Dead ones – lots of them – hung around his neck. He wore a top hat and held a long staff topped with a skull. Obviously one of the mystics from the square. His companion was a boy about Jack's age, who held something shiny in his hand.

"You did not draw any attention to yourself? Left nothing behind?" the old man asked.

"Only a bronze ship."

Everyone from the *Barnacle* heard *that* part. Tumen looked over anxiously.

The old mystic cackled, then clapped the boy on the shoulder. The boy's hand shot out and revealed that he was clutching an amulet.

Tumen's face went white, then darkened with anger. Jack raised an eyebrow at him: *what?*

Tumen pointed at the amulet wordlessly, shaking with rage.

Jack squinted, taking a better look at it. It

had a sun design in the centre, and what looked like three empty settings around the edges. . . it was the treasure the Xitami had entrusted to Tumen's people! It was right here!

"Didn't know the mission would be quite *this* easy," he said, putting aside his bowl of stew. "The blasted amulet has practically landed in our laps!"

He leaped up and drew his rusty old sword, raising it threateningly in front of the boy and the mystic.

The two were caught off guard and didn't have time to draw any weapons of their own – if they had any. Jack lunged at the boy, hoping to grab the amulet quickly and be on his way without causing too big a scene. He hit with the flat of his sword, not wanting to cut the boy, just hoping to knock the amulet out of his hand.

*Clang!*

The boy turned his hand out, blocking the sword with the amulet. There was a strange noise, like a hiss, and the stink of something burning. Jack watched in surprise as a reddish-gold colour swallowed his sword from where it touched the amulet up. In less than a second his sword had been turned into bronze.

It was much heavier than before, and the unexpected weight pulled Jack's hand down.

"Well, we'll finish this the old-fashioned way," he said cheerfully, letting it drop and putting up his fists.

Fitzwilliam joined him and Jean rolled up his sleeves, ready for a good rumble. A still-angry Tumen pulled out his obsidion knife.

Jack tried to grab the amulet. The boy pulled it back at the last minute, slamming his other fist into Jack's side. Jack doubled over in pain as Jean dived at the boy's legs, trying to tackle him to the ground. The boy shot his hands out wildly, trying to keep his balance. Jack recovered himself and lunged forward again – and was rewarded by being slammed in the face by the amulet.

*Clonk.*

His jaw shook with a head-shattering pain. It felt like a tooth had been knocked clear out of his mouth. Yep – there was that burning, metallic taste of blood. Not the first time he had lost a tooth, but this felt like a whole row of them from one side of his mouth!

Jack tried to run his tongue over the hole where his tooth had been. Then he realized that the tooth was still there. The acrid taste wasn't just metallic – it *was* metal. Forgetting the fight for a moment, he panicked and turned to look at his reflection in a nearby window. He gasped. A row of metal teeth shone out among his other sort-of-white ones. The boy – or the amulet – had turned it to bronze!

Jean, Tumen and Fitzwilliam had taken over where Jack left off. They had managed to wrestle the boy to the ground. Arabella crept up behind the mystic, raising her soup bowl over his head. But just as she was about to bring it down on his skull, he suddenly raised his hands in the air and shouted some thing in a language none of the friends knew.

All the dead snakes around his neck came alive.

Arabella jumped back as they began writhing and hissing, snapping at everyone who came near them.

Taking advantage of Fitzwilliam's and Jean's surprise, the boy slithered out of their grasp and leaped up. The old man grabbed him by the shoulder and pulled him close.

Two of the snakes began gasping. It looked as if they were regurgitating prey: two round objects worked their way up their necks. The old man put his hands out and the twin snakes each vomited a pearly white egg into his hands.

With another cry, the man raised the eggs above his head – and then smashed them to the ground.

They exploded with a cloud of smoke and the stench of rotten eggs. The crew of the *Barnacle* fell back, eyes stinging from the sulphurous cloud. When they were able to see again, the boy and the old man had gone.

"There goes the amulet," Tumen said sadly. "*Again*."

"Who in the 12th ring of Davy Jones's Locker was *that*?" Jack demanded.

"That," Jean said, "was Madame Minuit."

# CHAPTER EIGHT

*E*veryone stared at Jean.

"Well," said Jack, recovering first, "awfully ugly for a woman. Especially the stubble, the broad shoulders, the Adam's apple *and* the fact that she looked, oh, nothing like a woman at all. I've seen female dockworkers who looked better. Come to think of it, I've seen some old *male* dockworkers who were prettier . . ."

"Madame can manifest herself in two different ways," Jean said, cutting Jack off.

His eyes narrowed, looking at the spot where she had been. Only a few wisps of foul-smelling smoke remained. "One is a hag-like man – that is what you saw here," Jean continued. "The other I have never seen."

"How can you be sure it was her?" Fitzwilliam asked.

"The serpents gave her away. They are her sign. Her trademark." Jean made his hand writhe like snakes.

"Oooooo, spoooooky," Jack said sarcastically.

"Now," Jack said, clapping his hands together, "did any of you lot happen to get a close look at the amulet? Or notice anything funny about it?"

The four other crew members were silent. Jack sighed impatiently.

"Tumen here said the amulet had a sun surrounded by three empty settings for

74

gems. Well, mates – don't be shocked when I tell you this and go running off in a frightened tizzy, but . . ." Jack lowered his voice to a whisper, ". . . *one of the settings was filled.*"

Arabella, Jean, and Tumen stared at Jack.

"So?" Jean asked.

"There was a piece of *bronze* in one," Jack said, holding up his thumb and forefinger to indicate its size. "About the size and shape of a pearl. *Shiny. Bronze.* Oh, and did I mention it was *bronze?*"

He casually tapped his tooth. One of the ones that was also shiny and bronze now.

Arabella got it first.

"Oh!" she said.

"Yeah, 'Oh'," Jack mimicked, rolling his eyes.

"The ship! With all those people . . . and your tooth . . ." Arabella continued.

"And your sword," Fitzwilliam added,

picking it up off the ground. He looked at it closely. "Pure bronze."

"The amulet must be powered by the gem," Tumen said, nodding. "A bronze gem is in it, so it turns everything bronze."

"But why *bronze*?" Jack muttered, giving his old sword a disgusted look. It might have been a rusty and old sword *before*, but now it was completely useless – who ever heard of a bronze sword? "I mean, what good is *bronze*?"

"Jack," Arabella said with smile, "the entire *world* used to use bronze. Before iron and steel. Swords, helmets, shields, armour, lances, cooking pots . . . in some parts of the world, they still use bronze today."

"You're not fooling?" Jack asked, surprised. He grabbed his sword back from Fitzwilliam, giving him a suspicious look.

"I wonder what would happen if we put in *un diamant*? A diamond?" Jean asked thoughtfully. "Would everything it touched turn to diamond?"

Tumen shook his head, not liking where this line of thinking was going. "My people know the amulet to be very dangerous, Jean. I do not think we should play with it. Or have you already forgotten what happened with the Sword of Cortés?"

Jean nodded, looking chastised. "It almost got us enslaved to the corrosive conquistador, Hernán Cortés."*

"No more magic, no more curses," Fitzwilliam agreed, maybe a little sadly.

"No, no, no. This is not like the Sword of Cortés, this is totally different. *Totally* different!" Jack said, trying to forget what he promised himself about curses and treasure, and treasure and curses, and cursed treasure. "What could possibly be so dangerous about

*In Vols. 1-4: *The Quest for the Sword of Cortés.*

turning things into bronze? It's as useful as . . . as . . . turning things into tin, mates. Maybe if you want to upgrade your grandma's old cooking pot, or there's a wooden chair you want to make less comfortable for some odd reason."

Arabella's eyes grew wide, thinking. "If we could find a gold gem the exact same size and shape, we could test it out . . ."

"It would be like what happened with King Midas!" Fitzwilliam said, getting excited. "Everything he touched turned to gold!"

"Yeah, and we all know how that one ended up, don't we?" Jack mumbled.

"Or maybe diamond!" Jean said again.

"Diamond stones, diamond chairs, whatever you want, then," Fitzwilliam said, grinning. "You could buy whatever ship on the sea you wanted, Jack!"

"I have a ship already," Jack said, waving his hand dismissively, then looking up cautiously to see if any of the crew noticed that he knew full well that the *Barnacle* was little more than a fishing boat.

"I could have my own place. My own tavern. Well, saints – my own country!" Arabella said dreamily. "I'd never have to answer to anyone again."

Tumen looked from one to another of his friends, growing more dismayed. It was as if once they worked out the power of the amulet, they all went a little mad. All they could think about was treasure as a means to control their own destinies. Again. No wonder his people feared and protected the amulet.

Jean saw the look on his friend's face. Instantly, he felt ashamed.

"Friends, we are not after the amulet for its magical power," he reminded them gently. "We need it to go back and clear Tumen's good name so he can go home again."

79

Everyone looked blankly at him, and then at Tumen.

"Oh. Right," Fitzwilliam said quickly.

"Absolutely," Arabella agreed, blushing.

"Yes, yes," Jack muttered.

Just then, Constance leaped up onto a barrel. Something dangled from her mouth. Arabella jumped back, expecting the cat's usual 'gift': a half-dead mouse or rat. But this time it was neither alive nor dead, nor a mouse. It was a tarnished bronze key, dangling from the end of a pink silk ribbon.

"Where did you get that, Constance?" Jean asked, taking it in his hand and giving his sister a pat.

Constance meowed and ran to the spot where she'd found the key. It was the very spot where the boy and Madame Minuit had disappeared.

# CHAPTER NINE

"*W*ell done, *ma soeur*," Jean said, scratching Constance under the neck. "You have found for us a clue."

"But what is it a key *to*?" Arabella asked, taking it and holding it up to examine it closely. It wasn't fancy, just a plain bronze skeleton key. It was old and burnished. The handle was in a heart shape, and the shaft was long and narrow. Made for a simple lock, there were only a couple of grooves on the shaft. "It could unlock anything."

"Perhaps it is the key to a chest," Fitzwilliam suggested. "A key to where Madame keeps her treasure, like the amulet."

"Oh, *that* makes a pile of sense," Jack said, shaking his head. "How convenient. The Madame – or Mr Madame – or whatever she is – just *happens* to drop the precious key to her precious chest of magical and *precious* treasures?"

"She did not look like the sort of woman who likes pink ribbons," Tumen pointed out. The others had to agree. The undead snakes and crazy-old-man disguise didn't seem to go with ribbon and lace.

"Maybe it is the key to a house," Jean suggested. "Where she is staying, or hiding out."

"Wonderful," Arabella said bitterly. She handed the key to Fitzwilliam so he could take a closer look. "How many houses are there in New Orleans? All we have to do is try each one."

As Fitzwilliam put out his hand to take the key, Jack slapped the boy's wrist and grabbed it himself.

He held it up to the light as Fitzwilliam began to bluster. Running his fingers along the shaft, he felt a bumpy, raised texture. He spat on his thumb and rubbed harder. After a moment some of the dirt and finish came off. He tilted it forward and squinted at it.

"'Auberge d'Orléans'," he finally was able to read. But he pronounced it *ow-hergie dor-lians*. "What's that supposed to mean?"

"*Auberge* is an inn," Jean explained. "It is the Inn of Orléans. They talked about building it while I lived here. I guess they have completed it now. I think it's a place for rich people. I have no idea where it is, though."

Jack sighed. "Right then, let's ask the friendly natives."

He put the key in his pocket and plastered a giant, friendly smile on his face. Unfortunately, the more normal-looking natives seemed to have left after the lunchtime rush. Most of the people who remained were more street mystics, indigents and people of questionable trade.

He chose a large woman in a bright-yellow dress having tea outside a small shop. From the back at least, she looked like an upright, wholesome citizen.

"Excuse me, madam," Jack said, giving her a sweeping bow. "I was wondering if you could possibly tell me the – *yergh!*"

The woman turned around expectantly. She had a full, black, curly beard.

"Yes?" she asked in a deep, husky voice. "Read your tea leaves?"

"Ah, no thank you, not today, I'm having coffee," Jack apologized, backing away.

A gentleman walked by, dressed appropriately, Jack thought, in a top hat and shiny polished boots. Jack took a moment to study him, though, to make sure.

"Excuse me, good sir," Jack said, pressing his hands together and bowing. "I was wondering if you could kindly . . ."

"Let your blood? Absolutely!" the man replied eagerly. He held up a syringe and a jar full of wet, black, squirming things. "Needle or leeches?"

Jack backed away slowly. "Terribly sorry. I thought you were someone else. Entirely. Without the, ah, sucky-things."

This was getting ridiculous. Where was a *gendarme*, or policeman, when you actually needed one? Jack stomped through the crowd of freaks and magicians. Then it was as if they parted, clearing a path before him. At the end of it was one of the most spectacular women he had ever seen. She was tall and had porcelain-white skin that fairly gleamed against the midnight-black dress that hugged her body. Her hair was blood red – so dark it looked almost black, and she wore beautifully gemmed netting over it. Trailing from her hand was a masquerade mask, green and spangled, with sparkling silver fangs.

She wasn't exactly normal, or what Jack was looking for. But she seemed slightly more reliable than his other options. And besides, she was gorgeous.

"Excuse me, madam," he began, as he stepped forward. "I was wondering if you could point me in the direction of the Auberge d'Orléans. And the quickest possible route there, if you could. I'm in a bit of a hurry."

The woman parted her lips in a beautiful smile.

"*Bon chance*," she said. "That is exactly where I am going. You can follow me there." Her accent was heavily French, not that different from the man at the docks who checked for the crew's papers.

Jack smiled cockily. He waved to the crew to come over. Everyone but Arabella looked relieved. She took one look at the beautiful woman and frowned. When she saw Fitzwilliam begin to straighten his jacket, she hit him.

The woman walked ahead with Jack, her hips swaying gracefully as she went. She cast sidelong looks at the five friends, and she bit her lip.

"The Auberge is . . . a . . . very *formal* place," she said as politely as she could.

The crew of the *Barnacle* looked at each

other. Only then did they notice how dirty their clothes were. Even the impeccable Fitzwilliam could have used a bit of a wash. It wasn't as if they'd had a chance to do laundry or freshen up since their adventures began! Jean tried to pat the dust off his shirt.

Constance, trotting along beside them, spat on the ground derisively. It almost seemed as if she *liked* being mangy and dirty.

"There is a masquerade tonight," the woman suggested. "You *might* be able to get in if you are in costume . . . and cleaned up a bit. But your dreadful old cat will never be allowed."

Constance arched her back and hissed at the woman. Jean scooped up his sister and hugged her defensively.

"Oh, leaving that thing behind won't be a problem," Jack said suavely, to the clear consternation of Jean. He gave a wink to his friends. "We have to get in . . . a cousin of mine, he's in the shipping business. Rum, of course. What else would it be? Rum and bananas. All over the world. *Huge* exporter. Tremendously well respected in New Orleans. Going to get us all jobs. Owes me, he does. But he's a bit of a hotshot, big fellow, you know the type, very 'hoity-toity'. We can't miss the appointment. *Hate* people like that, don't you? No leeway at all."

He gave the woman his most winning smile.

She smiled back.

"Well, I am a *fairly* well-respected member of New Orleans society," she said with a wink. "Perhaps I can assist you."

"Most grateful, beautiful lady," Jack said with another bow. Then he dropped back and whispered to his friends. "Did you see that? She is absolutely crazy about me. Ain't no crime in being charming and handsome."

Arabella rolled her eyes.

It turned out to be a short walk to the hotel, which was just as grand as Jean had thought, with gaslights, tall columns, a red carpet leading in and a very impressive-looking doorman with a long, grey cape and matching cap. He gave the crew of the *Barnacle* a disgusted once-over. Then he saw the woman, and his attitude immediately changed.

"*Bon soir, madame*," he said politely, bowing.

"*Bon soir*," she swiftly said back. Then she spoke at length to him, continuing in French. She gestured at the crew. When they had finished, the woman turned and nodded at Jack.

"You may follow me."

The doorman made a big show of stepping back so it looked as if he had nothing to do with them as they filed past – until Jean tried to walk by, Constance still in his arms.

The doorman shook his head. The unwashed, yes. But cats – no. There had to be a limit somewhere. He held out his arm to stop them – but was careful not to get too close to Constance. It was as if he were afraid of getting some horrible disease from the nasty-looking thing.

The woman in black gave him a smile and shook her head. "*Oui, le chat aussi,*" she said, snapping her fingers.

Grudgingly, the doorman let them go. Fitzwilliam gave him a look – if it had been on his father's estate, the man would have been fired for letting such riff-raff in.

"She is a very powerful woman," the doorman explained, shrugging. "What can I do?"

Inside the hotel, a grand ball was in progress. Miles of thick red-and-black velvet was draped over everything: chairs, tables, walls and even doors. The long hall they went down had mirrored walls and was hung with chandeliers. Flickering shimmers of light illuminated partygoers all in costume, glasses of champagne in their hands. They wore elegant masks of incredible design: horned demons, haloed angels, feathered birds, petalled flowers, golden moons and things too strange to describe.

Arabella tried not to gape. Fitzwilliam looked a little uncomfortable. The ball was too much like the ones he had been forced to go to at home, when his father was trying to marry him off.

The woman snapped her fingers. From out of nowhere an attendant in a black-and-red cape appeared. He presented her with a bag filled with masks. She smiled and picked through them, carefully choosing five.

"You must wear these," she told the crew of the *Barnacle*. She gave Jack a golden mask with a sharp, pointed nose. Delighted, Jack put it on. It would be easy to sneak around the hotel in disguise. For Arabella there was a fiery red one adorned with feathers that swept back and up over her ears. Fitzwilliam got a more traditional one, white with a fake tricorn hat above, black diamonds around the eyes. It went perfectly with his blue jacket and shiny black shoes. Jean and Tumen wore matching devilish masks, complete with horns and pointed eyebrows.

"Very handsome," Arabella said approvingly.

"This is the stuff, mates," Jack said, staring at his reflection in a nearby tarnished mirror. "We'll blend in perfectly."

"I must go now. Good luck finding your cousin," the woman said with an elegant wave of her hand. She turned away and put on her own mask. As she walked into the room, the crowd parted before her. Tumen and Fitzwilliam watched her go, a little sadly.

"Look at that," Jean said, grabbing Jack. At the far end of the hall was an old woman all in green, wearing what looked like snakes around her neck! They were skinnier and longer than the old man's, but still . . . it *had* to be Madame Minuit.

Jack frowned and silently pointed. Jean's jaw dropped. There were two *other* people in the hall, also wearing snakes. One was a younger woman; she laughed and tapped a cane with a carved viper twirling up it. Another was a man all in yellow with a yellow mask and a belt that looked as if it was made from coiled snakes.

"I don't know if any of these is our man, er, woman, um, mate," Jack said, "but the company we are keeping at this here party is making me a little bit uneasy, you know, not being able to really see the partygoers' eyes and all that."

Jack leaned in closer to his crew. "Let's split up and find out which – if *any* – of these colourful characters is Madame Minuit."

# CHAPTER TEN

$\mathcal{J}$ack headed towards the first woman they had spotted, at the far end of the ballroom. Jean and Tumen crept up on the man with the snake belt, and Fitzwilliam and Arabella approached the lady with the cane. With all of the partygoers in the ballroom, it was easy to mingle and hide among them.

The woman with the blood-red hair who led them to the hotel stepped up to a podium. The crowd began applauding. The crew of the *Barnacle* hastily did the same, trying to blend in as much as possible.

"Welcome, everyone," the woman said in a rich voice that carried well, "to our annual *Masquerade Noir*."

With the audience's attention elsewhere, the five friends began to inch towards their targets. Arabella took a deep breath. The woman with the snake on the cane had a small purse hanging off her wrist, just about the right size for an amulet. With Fitzwilliam looking nervous, Arabella started to sneak her hand into the purse, just as she had seen pickpockets do back in Tortuga. Almost there . . .

"Ah-ha!" Jack's voice rang out. The old woman *he* had been tailing was right in front of him. The telltale gleam of a silvery amulet shone against her neck.

Arabella jerked her hand back quickly so as not to be noticed. Tumen and Jean also jumped away from their man. Fitzwilliam's hand went to his sword. Constance hissed.

The entire room turned to look at Jack.

So did the gorgeous woman who had let them in. But unlike the rest of the partygoers, she did not look shocked or surprised. In fact, she looked *satisfied*. It was almost as if she knew something like this was going to happen. As if this was the reason she had brought the crew of the *Barnacle* to the hotel!

"*J'accuse!*" Jack cried triumphantly at the old woman with the amulet. He spun her around roughly and presented her to the crowd. "This vile, this powerful – well, okay, this rather frail-looking old woman . . . might not look so threatening. Oh, no, not in the least. But, ladies and gentlemen, do *not* let her fool you! She *is* vile and powerful. Look at her snakes . . ." He grabbed one to hold it up. It fell limply in his hand, soft and tickly. What he and Jean both thought were snakes were actually just dark-green boas. "Okay, well, they *look* like snakes. Obviously, they're *meant* to be snakes. I mean, come on, from a distance . . . ?" Jack said, almost stuttering.

Arabella sighed as Jack prattled on. Fitzwilliam shook his head.

"We've been following her, you see," he explained to the confused-looking audience. He pressed his hands together like a teacher and strode back and forth. "All the way from the Yucatán, where she used weird little dolls to make a poor old witch doctor sick . . ."

"He is not a witch doctor," Tumen mumbled. "He is my great-grandfather."

Jack shot him an exasperated look. "Okay, even worse. She made an old great-*grandfather* sick. Just to take his amulet. His powerful, magical amulet. That turns things into bronze. Well, all right, I realize that doesn't sound *that* powerful," he admitted. "I didn't really think so, either. I mean, it's not like it turns things into gold, or even chocolate. But it did turn an entire ship into – ah – *bronze*, and well, LOOK! THE AMULET!"

He ended his speech quickly, grabbing a necklace from the woman and holding it up. "You are all in the presence of the mysterious and greatly feared Madame Minuit!"

The crowd was silent.

Then the woman with the blood-red hair laughed.

"Are you sure that is the *right* amulet, Jack?" she purred.

Jack frowned. He looked at the golden disc in his hand. It actually looked nothing like the amulet they were searching for. It had none of that piece's elegance. Instead, it was filled with ugly, big red-and-green gems.

The sort of jewellery a crazy old rich woman would wear.

"Wait, how did you know my name?" he asked, suddenly realizing what she had said.

The woman just laughed again and clapped her hands. "Let us help you find your amulet. Perhaps it's that one over there . . . or the one Mademoiselle Calais is wearing over by the door? Or maybe that one?"

With nasty leers and smiles, many others in the crowd pulled out gleaming amulets. They waved them tauntingly. None of the amulets was quite right – some were square, some had moons on them, some had a different number of empty places where gems would go.

"Jack . . ." Arabella said, worriedly.

"Perhaps Monsieur Voiture is wearing it," the woman on the podium continued. "Or perhaps you are looking for *mine*!"

She triumphantly pulled out an amulet of her own. A *stolen* amulet of her own – with seven points, four filled with jade, two empty settings, and one with a bronze gem in it!

"Well, I guess you would be the lovely Madame Minuit, then," Jack said weakly.

She threw her head back and laughed a terrible, hissing laugh. "Welcome to your first *masquerade noir*, my dear new friends. Now, let's see if you can survive the experience!"

The old woman with the snake boas grinned at Jack and slowly lowered her mask. Instead of the frail-looking old biddy Jack expected, her eyes glowed yellow like a snake's and her cheeks were scaly. The muscles on her face and head stood out as if she were possessed. She hissed.

The man in front of Jean and Tumen threw his mask down. His face was chalky, and the whites of his eyes were red. His hands were clawed with long, yellow fingernails.

"*Mon dieu*," Jean whispered. "He is possessed! JACK! They are all possessed by Madame Minuit!"

Around the room, everyone was taking off their masks. They all had crazed faces and stricken, leering mouths.

"Thank you for the update there, mate," Jack called back bravely. "I think I could have figured that out myself."

And then the possessed attacked.

"Get her! Get Madame Minuit!" Jack shouted, waving his hands frantically. "She's controlling them!"

Easier said than done. Jean and Tumen had their backs to each other as a group of partygoers closed in. Tumen pulled out his obsidian knife.

"Remember – these are normal people under a spell," Jean cried, punching the man with the snake belt as he lunged at them. "Try not to hurt them too much!"

Tumen sighed and put his knife away. Then he kicked the feet out from underneath the person closest to him.

It was too crowded in the ballroom for Fitzwilliam to draw his sword. He put a protective arm in front of Arabella and head-butted a gaunt old man who was drooling black ooze. Arabella thought fast, grabbed the snake-cane from the woman they had been trailing and clocked him with it.

But for each one of the fiends defeated, there were five more possessed partygoers behind them.

Jack knocked one down and leaped over him, kicking another one in the face as he went. A third stuck out a nasty clawed hand, and Jack spun out of the way, keeping his fist out and taking down two more.

And they kept coming.

With a final shove, Jack made it up to the podium. He ran forward and reached out to grab the amulet.

The woman held up her hand. A snake came down from around her neck and slithered daintily down her arm. It raised its head and hissed at Jack.

Suddenly, he couldn't move. It was as if he had no control over his own legs.

He watched in horror as more snakes slithered up and around the woman's neck and down around her arms.

She strode forward calmly, the snakes hissing and flicking their tongues out as she went. The possessed crowd made room for her as she passed by, bowing.

Arabella raised a pitchfork from a nearby hearth to strike Madame Minuit – but two of the snakes rose up and hissed, one at Arabella, one at Fitzwilliam. They, too, were then frozen in place. Fitzwilliam's arm was stuck reaching for his sword. Arabella opened her mouth to scream but couldn't.

Madame Minuit made for Jean and Tumen next. Two more snakes hissed, and the boys couldn't move, either.

The crowd gibbered and cackled. Madame Minuit looked around the room, smiling smugly. The crew of the *Barnacle* struggled in vain against the spell holding them. Madame Minuit approached Jack and waved her hand in front of him. Suddenly he could move his mouth – but nothing else.

"*Tell me*," she said in a hypnotic voice, "why you chase after the power of the amulet."

Jack felt himself compelled to speak.

"The *whole* story?" Jack asked.

"If you please," Madame Minuit said sinisterly.

Unfortunately for Madame, Jack was never at a loss for words.

"Well, you see," he began with relish, "it all started on the coast of the Yucatán. You know: white sandy beaches, yellow sun, blue skies, tall palm trees. That sort of thing. A veritable paradise. Actually, a *real* paradise. Great place to get away, if you know what I mean. For a holiday or a long rest from the job. The food there is simply marvellous, too. The natives have this amazing way with iguana. And dog. Well, maybe not so much with dog. They have this *delightful* cream sauce . . ."

Growing impatient, Madame Minuit had one of her snakes hiss in Jack's face. Jack quickly became silent.

"It is obvious you have no idea about the *real* power of the amulet," she said dramatically, stroking one of her snakes on the head.

"Of course we do," Jack cut in, fighting the spell. "It goes around turning things into bronze. Big deal! Bronze. Puh!"

Madame Minuit looked irritated. He had interrupted her big moment.

"It may 'turn things into bronze' as you say, in its *current* state," she said acidly, "but it is also the key to the City of Gold!"

This City of Gold business again!

"I am sorry, my friends," she went on, "but you have become too great a threat to the amulet – and me. You leave me no choice. I must turn you over to the serpents."

Four large snakes slithered down her body and out to Jean, Tumen, Arabella and

Fitzwilliam. They raised themselves up and swayed back and forth. Madame Minuit held her arm up near Jack. A snake raised its head and bared its fangs, preparing to strike.

# CHAPTER ELEVEN

"*Er*," Jack said, cross-eyed from staring at the snake before him. He desperately tried to move, to fall down, to do anything to get out of its path. But it was no use. He was still paralysed. The snake reared back and opened its jaw.

Suddenly, Madame Minuit began shaking. Her hands flew to her neck and she screamed. The snakes all started writhing with her, pulling back from their intended victims.

Jack lurched to the side as he was released from the spell. He caught himself and leaped up, sword out. The rest of the crew of the *Barnacle* also shook themselves awake, stepping quickly away from the snakes.

Madame Minuit fell to her knees. Behind her was the boy they had seen her with before, back in the market. The one who originally had the amulet. He held a weird little doll with red hair and a black dress – a miniature Madame Minuit! He twisted its head and neck. Madame Minuit twisted and writhed in agony.

Constance poked her head out from behind the boy's legs and meowed cautiously. The key hung around her neck.

"What . . . ?" Jack began to ask. Why was the boy, who was Madame Minuit's partner in crime, now turning against her? Why did Constance have the key they had found earlier? And *why* was the wretched cat standing with the boy?

Fitzwilliam and Arabella were equally speechless.

"Get out of here!" the boy urged them desperately. "Run!"

"Let's not look a gift *snake* in the mouth, mates. Run!" Jack shouted. But before he turned, he grabbed the amulet and pulled it off Madame Minuit's neck.

"NO!" she screamed, clawing at him. The boy gave the doll one last good twist before taking to his bare feet after Jack. Constance was close behind.

Once more reunited, the crew of the *Barnacle* began to fight their way out of the ballroom. It was even worse than before. Although the partygoers were just as crazed and vicious, they were now also stumbling around and smashing the furniture. Madame

Minuit's hold on them had weakened – now they just wanted to destroy *everything*. And that included Jack and his friends.

"Look out!" Arabella shouted as a tall man in a top hat tried to rip Jack's eyes out. Jack threw an arm up, blocking the man's hand. The amulet swung out at the end of its chain and hit the man in the chest. Instantly, it turned him into bronze.

There was no time to stare. There were still what seemed like several hundred creepy possessed men and women between them and the way out.

As Jack and his friends made their way to the door, the fighting grew more intense. The amulet pitched around violently, knocking into possessed men and women, chairs, walls . . . and once, almost Fitzwilliam. Everything it touched turned to bronze.

When they finally made it to the exit, the

amulet struck the door frame as Jack ran through. Behind him, reddish metallic gold crept up the walls and swallowed the floors and the windows. The entire hotel was being turned into bronze.

"Hold that thing close to you!" the boy yelled at Jack as they ran through the streets.

Unfortunately, the suggestion came a moment too late. As they rounded a corner, the amulet knocked into a lamppost.

Jack watched in horror as the cobbled street below him began to turn into bronze. Houses, buildings, side streets, walls, alleys, flowerpots . . .

The crew didn't stop running until they made it back to the dock and onto the *Barnacle*. Only once they were safely aboard did they turn to look back at New Orleans. The entire city gleamed dully under the light of the rising moon.

"Oh, wonderful," Jack said sarcastically. "A City of Bronze. The stuff that dreams are made of."

Fortunately, unlike the boat they had found in the gulf, it looked like people – and animals – hadn't been turned. They were walking, looking very confused. And falling a lot. Apparently bronze walkways were much more slippery than stone ones.

"Hold it!"

It was the boy who had been with Madame Minuit. He was trying to board the *Barnacle*, too. Fitzwilliam stood with one foot on the rail of the boat, his sword point on the boy's chest. "What, pray tell, do you think you are doing?" he demanded.

"Please," the boy begged. His blue eyes were wide with terror. "Let me come with you! I can't hold her forever – when she sees what I've done she'll kill me!"

"Why should I let you on board?" Jack asked. "Why should I trust you? You obviously stole the amulet from Tumen's witch doctor . . ."

"Great-grandfather," Tumen corrected, somewhat tiredly.

". . . and used that weirdo dolly-thing to make him sick," Jack continued. "*And* you turned that entire ship and its crew into bronze!"

"But I just saved you from Madame, didn't I?" the boy pointed out. He kept looking over his shoulder, as if expecting her to appear at any moment.

"Yes. But then, you also tried to *kill* us back in the square!" Jack countered.

Jack looked him angrily in the eyes. The boy really did look terrified. And he didn't really fit the role of 'partner' to the beautiful Madame Minuit. His feet were bare, his trousers worn and torn, his face dirty. He was little more than a street urchin. Maybe some poor boy she had kidnapped to do her dirty work.

"*THERE THEY ARE!*"

A crowd of fancy-dressed people in masks had gathered at the foot of the dock. Dockworkers and sailors looked confused at their sudden appearance. The harbourmaster strode up to them, demanding to know what they were doing.

"This is property of the port of *Nouvelle Orleans!*" he said, flustered. "Do you have your papers–"

A possessed man hissed and head-butted him in the skull. The harbourmaster fell like a sack of wet mud into the river.

"Jack," Arabella said worriedly.

"I am completely on it," Jack said. Rather than taking the time to carefully untie and coil up the ropes, he pulled out his sword and brought it down on them. The lines were severed, and the *Barnacle* was free of the dock. "Hmm, maybe a bronze sword isn't all that bad, after all," he said thoughtfully, looking at his blade.

Jean and Tumen leaned over, giving the dock a good shove. They pushed off, just as the first of the crowd reached the boat. One man overshot and fell into the water, letting out a horrible, gurgling scream.

The boy looked around him and made a decision. Possessed people behind him on the dock, a rapidly retreating boat before him in the water . . .

He leaped.

His feet just cleared the water, the drowning man who had just fallen off the dock reaching at his ankles. The boy landed on the edge of the deck, barely making it.

The possessed crowd parted. Madame Minuit stepped forward, dozens of snakes wrapped around her upraised arms. They hissed loudly and evilly.

The crew of the *Barnacle* shrank back.

"Don't worry," the boy told them. "She is too far away for her snakes to have any power over you. We're safe. For now."

Jean shuddered, then forced himself to turn and begin hauling up the sails. Tumen and Fitzwilliam joined in making the boat ready. Jack took the wheel, spinning it hard to get them away.

"Go where you will!" Madame Minuit shouted triumphantly at them. "But the City of Gold is wherever gold has lived!"

That was almost exactly what Mam had said. What did they both know about the City and the amulet? It was something to think about . . . later. Right now, it was time to concentrate on escaping.

The *Barnacle* drifted away from the port of New Orleans. The now-bronze city gleamed faintly in the moonlight. And Madame Minuit's laughter echoed over the water.

# CHAPTER TWELVE

Arabella wiped her brow and muttered something most unladylike. Jean and Tumen slumped to the deck, and Fitzwilliam breathed a sigh of relief as they all watched New Orleans grow smaller on the horizon.

"Mighty close one, that was," Jack said grimly.

"What would have happened if the snakes had bitten us?" Tumen asked, curious.

The boy they had picked up was still standing at the edge of the boat, staring at the receding shoreline as if he couldn't quite believe he was free.

"It would have made you all slaves to the Madame. Just like the partygoers. Just like *me*," he said softly. He shook his head, clearing it of morbid thoughts. He turned to face the crew. "The effect wears off after a time. She has to have them keep biting you." He pulled up his sleeve. Up and down his arm were dozens of pairs of little bite marks. Some were fresh, some were scabbed over, but most still oozed with venom and blood.

"Oh, me saints and heavens," Arabella said. "That woman is a monster!"

"You don't have to tell me," the boy said ruefully, covering his arm up again. "She kept me locked up in a room in the hotel, and used me to do all her dirty work. Like stealing the amulet. I'm sorry about your great-grandfather," he said seriously to

Tumen. "I didn't have a choice. It was her, doing it through me. I didn't do it of my own accord."

"Will he be all right?" Tumen asked anxiously. He handled the Mam doll, which he had been carrying safely in his pocket.

The boy nodded. "He should be fine, now that neither I nor Madame has the doll."

"But what about the ship?" Jack demanded. "The . . . you know . . ." He took his hands off the wheel and waved his arms . . . "Big? Bronze? In-the-middle-of-the-gulf ship?"

The boy frowned. "That was more of Madame's orders. She had me search the ship for the Bronze Bullet. That is what that gem is called." He pointed at the amulet, which now hung safely around Jack's neck. "Captain Henshaw was the last person known to have it. It's the first stone in the amulet, the one you need to activate its power. Madame Minuit made another doll of him so I could get him to tell me where the bullet was hidden, and then steal it."

"All right, then," Arabella said, frowning. "But why *leave* the dolls? Didn't ye want to hang on to them? Didn't ye just say that they lose their power if they fall out of the maker's hands?"

"It's true," the boy said, nodding at Jean. "But I dropped them on purpose. As the snakebites begin to heal, the spell wears off. During those times – when Madame Minuit had little power over me – I formed a plan. I left the dolls as clues during those moments of clarity, so someone would find them and know it was Madame Minuit doing all of these horrible things. I hoped that someone would find the dolls and come after her. And you did."

"I like the way you think, mate," Jack said,

warming up to the newcomer. Then Jack pointed at Constance and the key around her neck. She hissed at him out of habit. "What about the key there?" Jack asked.

"It's to the hotel room she kept me in. I dropped it, too, on purpose, when Madame Minuit was transporting us out of the market," the boy explained, grinning at his own cleverness. "I hoped you would come and find me. Somehow, this . . . cat? . . . got hold of it and slipped it under my door. Beautiful thing, whatever she is."

He smiled and scratched Constance under the chin. Constance purred.

"Okay, what are *you* drinking, and where can I get some?" Jack asked.

"Beautiful?" Arabella asked doubtfully, exchanging a look with Fitzwilliam. The mangy cat purred with pleasure, exposing her crooked, yellow teeth. About time someone respected her natural beauty.

Jean beamed. "My sister! Good job!"

"I had stolen one of Madame's dolls earlier, during one of those times when I was myself again, those moments of clarity," the boy continued. "I dressed it like her. So when I came to the ballroom I was able to use her own power against her to free you."

"Right clever of you!" Jack said.

They were *all* impressed by the young boy's ingenuity and perseverance. Imagine putting together a plan for escape while still under the spell of a sorceress!

"What's yer name, lad?" Jack asked, holding the wheel with one hand and sticking out his other hand to shake.

"Timothy. Tim. Tim Hawk, sir," the boy said.

The crew of the *Barnacle* shrugged. Never

heard of him. But Jack definitely enjoyed being called sir. He was pretty sure he was going to like the newest member of his crew.

"Well, Timothytimtimhawksir," Jack said cheerfully, "Now that we've got your ex-employer's amulet, we can take it back to Tumen's village in the Yucatán. Tumen will once again be accepted by his friends and family, we'll have a strong ally on the coast, the amulet will be safe, and everyone will live happily ever after."

Tumen smiled in gratitude. And maybe a little in surprise – was Jack really giving up a mystery, magic and, most of all, *treasure*? Just to help his friend out? Jack wasn't a bad guy, but this was unlike him.

"Er, that's everyone happily ever after except for the good people of that there city," Jack added, pointing at the coast. "New

Orleans will have to suffer the sad fate of being transformed into the not-really-glamorous City of Bronze. Not one for myths *or* the history books, I'd wager."

Tim studied him curiously. "You're just going to give the amulet back? You're not the least bit interested about what the other stones in the amulet will do?"

Jack thought about it for a moment. Really and truly. He searched his soul.

"No," he finally said flatly. The determined look in his eyes convinced his crew.

The next morning, the *Barnacle* sailed steadily through the Gulf of Mexico . . . and wound up again passing the bronze ship. A little more of the bronzed water around it had rusted and cracked off into the sea.

Tim stared at it for a long while. When

Fitzwilliam went to get him for his turn at bilge pumping, the boy took a deep breath.

"I didn't mean to," he apologized. "I didn't *want* to. All those people . . ."

Fitzwilliam looked up at the bronze man at the wheel.

"It wasn't your fault. Perhaps we can find a way to turn them back," he said, clapping the boy on the shoulder.

*"CREW OF THE BARNACLE!"* a thunderingly loud voice called out, seemingly from the air itself.

The crew turned around. They had all been so busy looking at the bronze ship that they never noticed the *wooden* ship that was coming up right behind them.

"Halt! Who goes there – oh, no . . ." Jack trailed off, exasperatedly. It wasn't just a boat. It was a galleon, huge and strong, with many, many cannons. It flew the Jolly Roger. A *pirate ship*. A nasty-looking one.

"Pirates, Jack!" Fitzwilliam said, hand to his sword.

"Your powers of observation never cease to amaze me," Jack said drily. He narrowed his eyes, scanning the ship. Each pirate's flag had something unique about it. Jack grabbed the nobleman's expensive spyglass and put his eye to it. Maybe he could work out *which* pirate he was dealing with by looking at his flag. "The skull and crossbones has two – er, cross-*flowers* below the skull!"

Just then, the captain came out to greet them.

*She* strode up the deck, resting one boot on the base of the bowsprit. The pirate was magnificent: tall, beautiful, strong, every bit the perfect captain. *And* she had a

fabulous hat. She drew a shiny, sharp sword. So did the 30 pirates behind her.

Jack swallowed. But he refused to be intimidated. By *anyone*.

"Okay, lassie, make this quick!" he called back. "We're kind of on a mission here with a bit of a tight schedule . . ."

"Watch your tongue, lad!" the woman bellowed back. Her long, auburn locks whipped in the wind. "Know that you're at the mercy of Captain Laura Smith!"

"You know, it's funny," Jack whispered to Fitzwilliam, "she looks a little bit like . . ."

"*MUM?!*" Arabella cried, running forward.

"Your mother is dead,"* Fitzwilliam reminded her gently. "Killed by the notorious pirate Left-Foot Louis. You must still be upset by

---

*Arabella recounted her mother's death in Vol 1: *The Coming Storm* and Vol 3: *The Pirate Chase*.

our recent ordeal. This . . . pirate . . . only *looks* like your mother."

This pirate, however, stared down at the deck in shock. Twin sets of brown eyes gazed at each other.

"*Arabella?*" the captain called out, a catch in her voice.

"Aye, it's her," growled a pirate from behind her. With the shuffle that was feared across the Caribbean, Left-Foot Louis stepped forward. The crew of the *Barnacle* gulped in shock. Louis glared at Arabella and gestured towards her mother. "And thanks to you, I must suffer on her crew for eternity!"

The members of the *Barnacle*'s crew stared at one another.

"Well," Jack said cheerfully, "here we go again . . ."

*Don't miss the next volume in the continuing adventures of Jack Sparrow and the crew of the mighty Barnacle!*

## Silver

As it turns out, Arabella's mother is alive and well, and living a pirate's life – alongside the feared captain Left-Foot Louis. Shocks abound as more is learned about the *Barnacle*'s new crewmate, Tim Hawk, and the crew faces their most dangerous foe yet – the powerful Mr Silverback. All this, plus the mystery of the amulet continues.